Young, Ed
You   The lion and the mouse

	DATE DUE		
MAR 17 '83	11		
JAN 3	Ramil		
FEB 06	Sal		

0.1

THE LION
AND THE MOUSE

AN ÆSOP'S FABLE
PICTURES BY ED YOUNG

Benn Book
COLLECTION

Published by Doubleday & Company Inc., Garden City, New York

First edition in the United States of America · Printed in England · Second Printing 1980
Library of Congress Cataloging in Publication Data
The Lion and the Mouse. **Summary:** Recounts the tale of the tiny mouse who helped the mighty lion when he became ensnared by hunters.
(1. Fables. 2. Animals – fiction) 1. AESOP 11. Young, Ed.
PZ8.1.L65 398.2452 (E) 79-1863
ISBN 0-385-15462-3 (Trade) · 0-385-15463-1 (Prebound)
Library of Congress Catalog Card Number LC-79-1863

A mouse

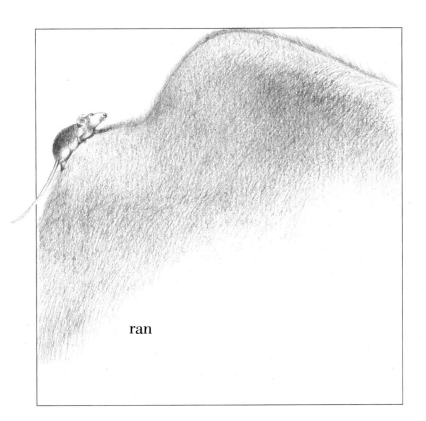

ran

over

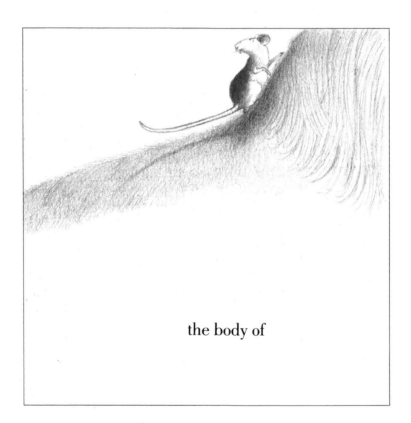

the body of

a sleeping lion.

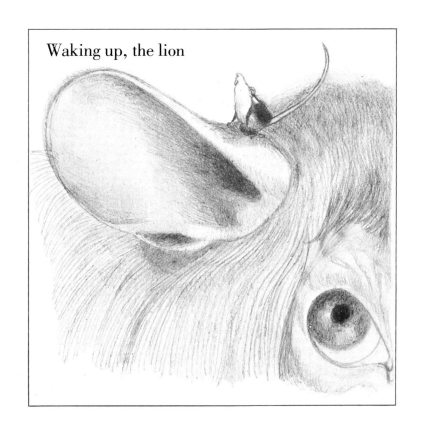

Waking up, the lion

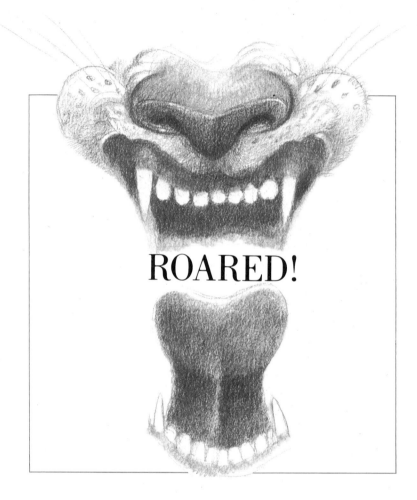

ROARED!

seized him

and was about to eat him.

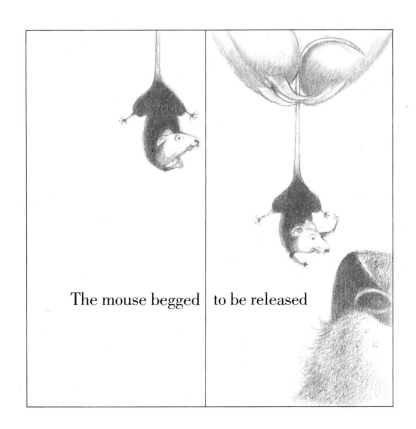

The mouse begged | to be released

and promised to repay the lion if he would spare him.

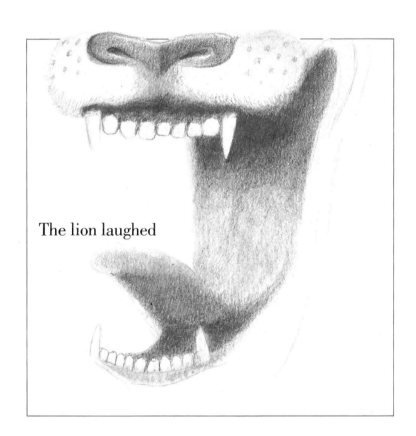

The lion laughed

and let him go.

Not long afterwards,

the mouse was able

to show his gratitude.

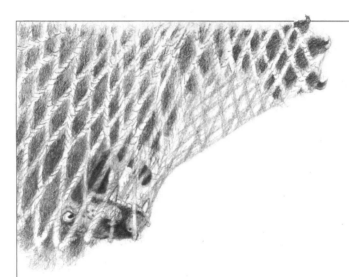

Captured by hunters in a net,

the lion was suspended by a rope.

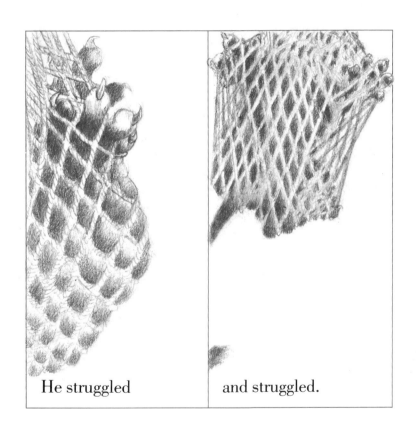

He struggled   and struggled.

The mouse heard his cry.

Running

to the spot

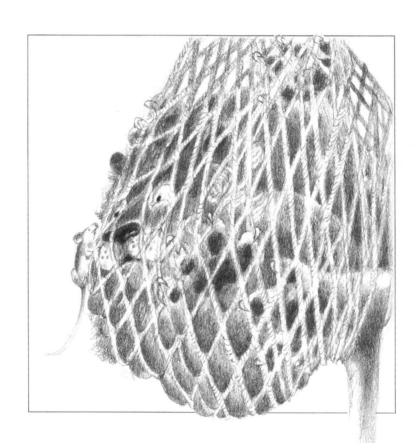

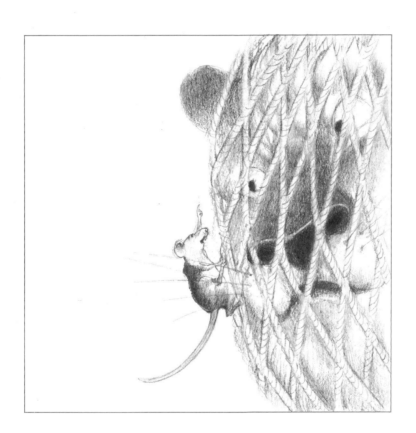

the mouse freed him

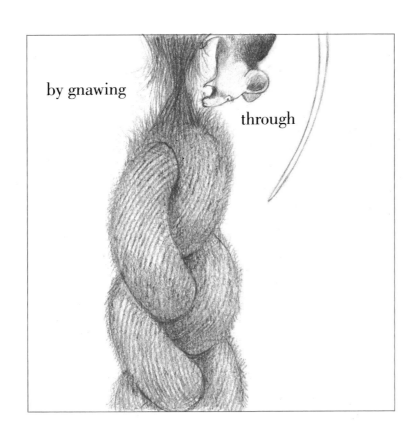

by gnawing

through

the rope.

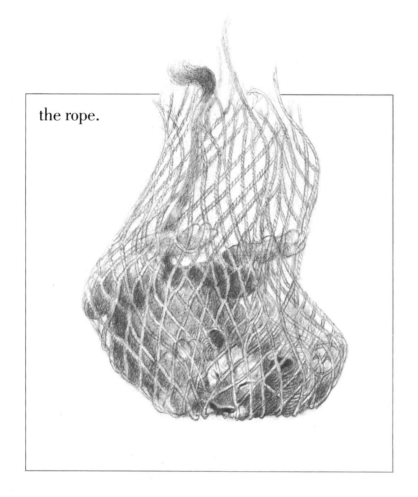

A change in circumstance can make
the strong weak and the weak, strong.